Itty-Bitty Ditch Kitty

Fulton Books
Meadville, PA

Published by Fulton Books 2023

ISBN 979-8-88505-620-5 (paperback)
ISBN 979-8-88505-622-9 (hardcover)
ISBN 979-8-88505-621-2 (digital)

Printed in the United States of America

Itty-Bitty Ditch Kitty

Sharon Kitto-Rienstra

In Louisiana, deep in the backwoods, where the air is hot, muggy, and really quite buggy, a young kitten wandered about—lost, lonely, and hungry. This little kitten was the most curious of cats, and it was this curiosity that he found himself in a great predicament. They say curiosity kills the cat, and well, it's not that bad, but he does have quite a story.

He was on a lovely porch with a lovely lady who would bring him saucers of milk. But something in the backyard was rustling in the distance, so he wandered to the curious noise, only to be led by another. He then found it fun to chase the leaves that the wind was blowing around teasingly.

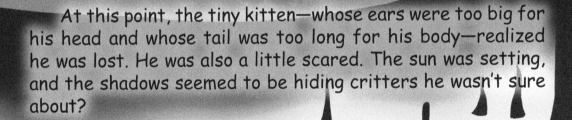

At this point, the tiny kitten—whose ears were too big for his head and whose tail was too long for his body—realized he was lost. He was also a little scared. The sun was setting, and the shadows seemed to be hiding critters he wasn't sure about?

1

Soon he heard snickering and giggles from the shadows. He eyed with his cat eyes some raccoons pointing at him, saying, "Look at his ears, they're huge," and they all laughed.

And from the boggy water, a couple of nutria rats were calling out to him, "Hey, what's with your tail? Why so long? Are you part snake?" And they all laughed.

Finally, the most maddening thing he heard was from a group of pesky field mice jeering at him, "You're a bug rug! Take a dip and get the fleas off your face, hahahaha!" They chortled. They knew cats did not like water.

"Leave him alone," said a slithering snake, sliding toward the small feline. "The fleas will be an added snack to this itty-bitty ditch cat of a kitten who will be my supper."

"Hahahahaha!" The swamp critters all laughed together and called him, "Itty-Bitty Ditch Kitty!" The little cat wondered why these critters were being so mean. He knew he had to get out of the swamp quickly.

Itty-Bitty looked at his reflection in the pond. His ears and tail *were* too big for his scrawny body, but he liked them anyway, especially his tail. He didn't think any other cat would have a tail this grand. Still Itty-Bitty felt awful. He was so hungry and scared. He looked up at a mighty mossy oak tree with beautiful moss dangling gracefully from its branches and decided he could hide up there till morning.

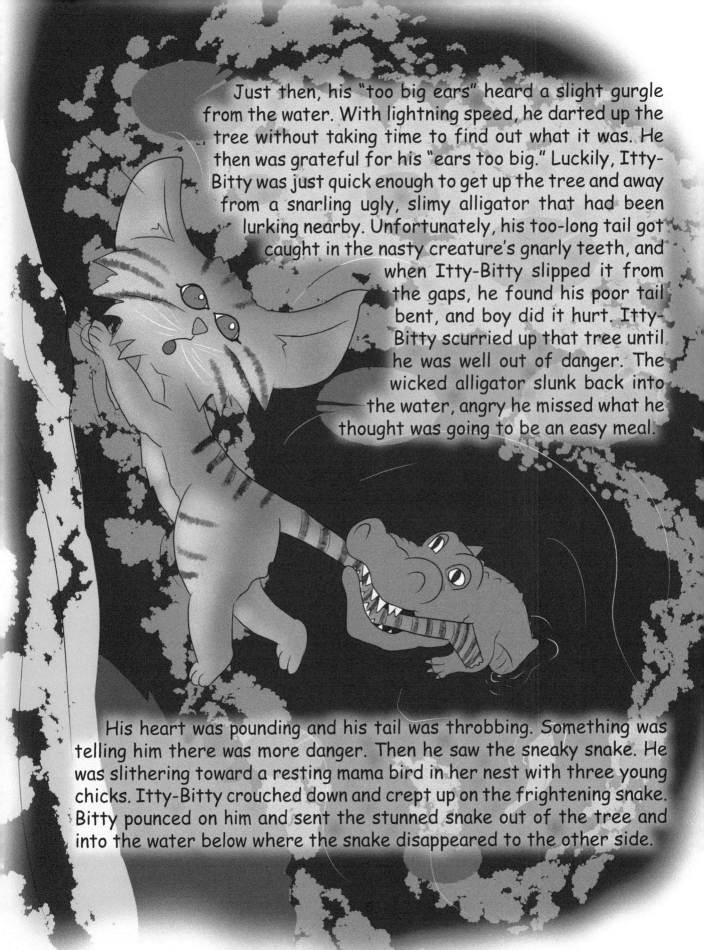

Just then, his "too big ears" heard a slight gurgle from the water. With lightning speed, he darted up the tree without taking time to find out what it was. He then was grateful for his "ears too big." Luckily, Itty-Bitty was just quick enough to get up the tree and away from a snarling ugly, slimy alligator that had been lurking nearby. Unfortunately, his too-long tail got caught in the nasty creature's gnarly teeth, and when Itty-Bitty slipped it from the gaps, he found his poor tail bent, and boy did it hurt. Itty-Bitty scurried up that tree until he was well out of danger. The wicked alligator slunk back into the water, angry he missed what he thought was going to be an easy meal.

His heart was pounding and his tail was throbbing. Something was telling him there was more danger. Then he saw the sneaky snake. He was slithering toward a resting mama bird in her nest with three young chicks. Itty-Bitty crouched down and crept up on the frightening snake. Bitty pounced on him and sent the stunned snake out of the tree and into the water below where the snake disappeared to the other side.

Mama Bird woke up, seeing the last part of the battle between Itty-Bitty and the wretched snake. She was speechless and frightened. So was Itty-Bitty. "Hello," he said, "don't be scared—that snake is gone." He realized she was guarding her chicks, not sure of his intentions. Cats and birds didn't usually make good friends.

"I'm not going to hurt you," he said. The small marsh wren sighed a great sigh of relief.

"Thank you for saving us," she said and offered Itty-Bitty some leftover worms she had from dinner with the chicks. Itty-Bitty gulped them down and immediately felt the tiredness the day had brought. He fell asleep next to her nest, and they all slept through the night.

The next morning, with the rising sun and a good night's sleep, Itty-Bitty felt much better. He saw that Mama Bird was already out gathering food for her chicks. He walked out on a limb to see if he could locate his home. He looked in every direction, but nothing looked familiar. He saw out to the west what appeared to be a building of some kind. He knew that people were usually inside of buildings, and his imagination ran away with him.

He thought of nice ladies there that would take him home and give him saucers of milk. Or a kindly older gentleman who would let him nap on his lap in chilly weather in front of a fire, or a family with lots of kids to play with...

All of a sudden, he heard a whoosh in the trees above that brought him out of his daydream. It was a mighty hawk looking for breakfast. He had seen Itty-Bitty on the limb below and started diving toward him. Itty-Bitty took his chances and jumped to the next tree, clinging to the moss hanging from it. He scurried to the inside of the tree, looking for a hiding place. The hawk above seemed to lose interest and flew away. Itty-Bitty's heart was once again pounding, and his tail still hurt from the previous day's adventure with the alligator. He knew he had to get out of this awful place. It was no good place for cats.

As luck would have it, a squirrel happened by, his mouth stuffed with acorns. "Excuse me," said Itty-Bitty politely, "can you tell me how to get out of this swamp?"

"Geh ouda hiss wamp?" the nutty squirrel asked as he was trying hard to remove the bounty from his mouth. "Get out of *this* swamp?" he said more clearly. "Are you mad? This place is great! Wouldn't leave it for anything. So no, I do not know any way out. You might want to ask the wise owls. They live in the biggest moss oak tree that way," and he pointed with his tail.

Way off in the distance, he saw the mightiest of trees. "That's really far away," Itty-Bitty said in an overwhelmed manner.

"Nah," said the nutty squirrel, "follow me, and I'll show you how to get around." He shoved the nuts back in his mouth, which made Itty-Bitty laugh. He liked this guy; he thought he was very kind to help a stranger. The self-assured squirrel grabbed hold of some moss vines and flew to the next tree.

"Wow," said Itty-Bitty, "that was amazing, but I don't think I can do that, and it's a long way down if I fall."

"You won't fall," said the nutty little squirrel who was determined to help Itty-Bitty. He could see that the marsh was indeed no place for him. Cats are for humans, and he would help get him to the owls no matter what.

"Don't be a scaredy cat, hahahaha—see what I did there? You're a cat, and you're scared, hahaha."

Itty-Bitty laughed a little at this and said, "Okay, here I go!"

"Just hold on tight with your claws and wrap that abnormally long tail around the moss, and you'll be fine! Oh, nice tail by the way, wish mine was that long," said the squirrel.

That was all Itty-Bitty needed to hear—he knew his tail wasn't *too* long and that it would serve him well one day, and that one day was today! With that thought, Itty-Bitty grabbed the vine, did what Squirrel told him, and launched himself from one tree to the next where Squirrel was waiting. But Nutty Squirrel didn't move, and Itty-Bitty landed smack on top of him. They both laughed and laughed.

11

"There—you see, not so hard, right?" said Squirrel. "Now just keep going, and you'll be there in no time."

"Thank you, Squirrel," said Itty-Bitty. His stomach growled angrily.

"No problem, kid," replied Squirrel, cracking one of the nuts and giving it to Itty-Bitty.

"Oh, thank you," said Bitty, chowing down the nut. Looking down to the ground, Bitty could see all kinds of nuts and showed Nutty Squirrel, who leaped with excitement.

"Oh, that will last for days, and the missus will be so happy—we just had little ones."

Itty-Bitty was glad to help Squirrel; he was a good friend.

"Well, kid, I gotta go. Best of luck to you. I'm sure the owls can help." And with that, Squirrel flew from one tree to the next, back to his home where his family waited.

"Goodbye—thank you again," Bitty called out after him.

So Bitty flew confidently from vine to vine, tree to tree with ease. He felt great flying through the air and saw a different, safer view of the swamp. It was actually quite beautiful from up high. Bitty could see the big tree approaching, and beyond that, the marsh appeared to be thinning. Bitty began to daydream again: nice ladies, saucers of milk...*BANG! FLASH!*

A thunderstorm was overhead. Bitty was so stunned by the calamity that he lost his grip on the vine and had loosened his tail trees ago. Down he fell hard with a *PLOP* at the bottom. Luckily, a mound of grass and marsh straw cushioned the small feline's fall, but it was still distressing. Itty-Bitty had to shake himself to clear his head. To make matters worse, it was starting to rain, and cats hate getting wet! He wanted to find a place to hide and rest for a minute, but Itty-Bitty saw the big tree, and with the weather turning bad, he could see all the owls heading for safety there.

So...with his big ears, long bent tail that still hurt badly, and a scrawny body full of fleas, he decided to hoof it the rest of the way to the tree. Itty-Bitty was feeling defenseless and lonely—not to mention hungry and weary. The trek was treacherous. Besides frightening thunder, lightning, and pouring-down rain, Itty-Bitty had to sneak by a den full of dozing foxes that surely would have enjoyed him for a quick snack—not to mention burrs and thorns poking him along the way. *Well, this is just great,* thought Itty-Bitty to himself. *What more could possibly happen? All I want is a nice home, with a nice lady who will give me SAUCERS OF MILK!* Itty-Bitty was angry. *Why is all of this sooo hard?* he wondered.

Finally, there was the big tree! The owls, along with the rest of the swamp animals, were resting quietly as the rain began to subside. "Excuse me," Bitty said quietly. Instantly, dozens of big owl eyes peered down upon him. "A friend of mine told me you might know a way to get out of this marsh. Can you help me?"

The owls looked at each other laughingly. One of the owls replied, "Forget it, runt, you'll never make it—it's too far and hard to get out of."

Another equally rude owl said, "If a hawk don't get you, a snake will. If a snake don't get you, the stink will." All the owls nodded and agreed unanimously. Then something terrific happened.

The biggest, most regal-looking owl came out of a notch in the tree, went to the end of the branch, and peered down at Itty-Bitty. "What brings you to my tree?" asked the old, wise-looking owl. He could see the small creature below was shivering, scared, and in a bad way.

"I...I was hoping you could tell me how to get out of this marsh...sir. I've had a terrible last few days, and I just want to find a home with a nice lady who will give me saucers of milk."

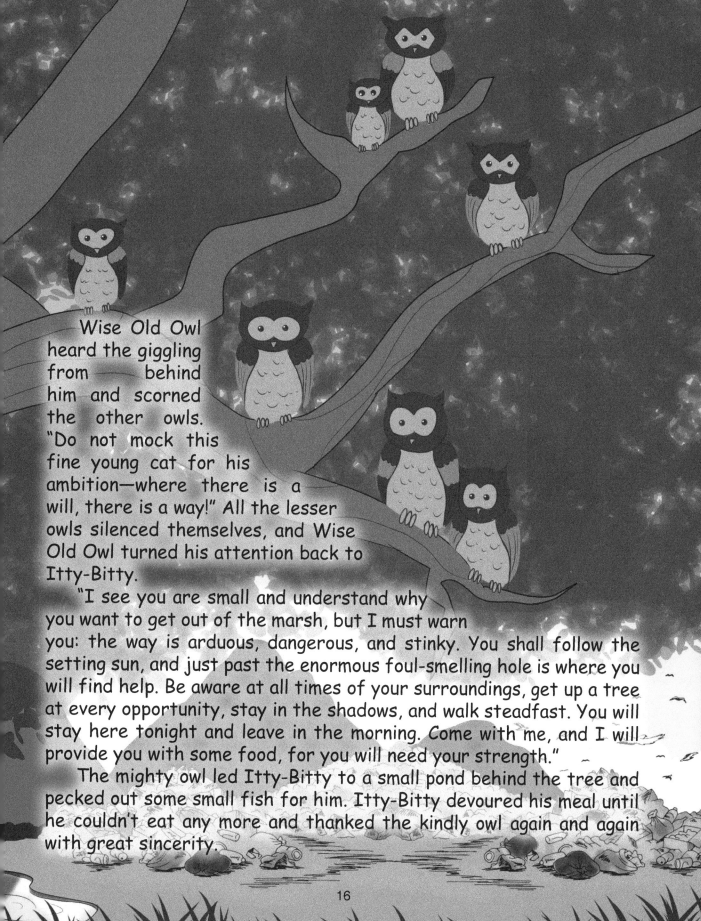

Wise Old Owl heard the giggling from behind him and scorned the other owls. "Do not mock this fine young cat for his ambition—where there is a will, there is a way!" All the lesser owls silenced themselves, and Wise Old Owl turned his attention back to Itty-Bitty.

"I see you are small and understand why you want to get out of the marsh, but I must warn you: the way is arduous, dangerous, and stinky. You shall follow the setting sun, and just past the enormous foul-smelling hole is where you will find help. Be aware at all times of your surroundings, get up a tree at every opportunity, stay in the shadows, and walk steadfast. You will stay here tonight and leave in the morning. Come with me, and I will provide you with some food, for you will need your strength."

The mighty owl led Itty-Bitty to a small pond behind the tree and pecked out some small fish for him. Itty-Bitty devoured his meal until he couldn't eat any more and thanked the kindly owl again and again with great sincerity.

Night came, and Itty-Bitty nestled into the bottom of the tree where he felt safe and secure for the first time in days. His tummy was full, and he fell fast asleep where he dreamed his wonderful dream of nice ladies and saucers of milk. When the morning came, Wise Old Owl guided Itty-Bitty to the edge of the enormous, gross-smelling pit.

Itty-Bitty's heart sank as he saw his destination so far away with mounds and mounds of trash and gook in the way. "Remember what I told you and you will be just fine. I know you will find your way, young man—you are determined and, despite your small appearance, have strength more than you realize." Bitty felt honored to hear these words. He thanked Wise Old Owl once again and went gingerly into the stench pit, weaving in and around giant mounds of mush and gook, ever aware of his surroundings like Owl instructed.

17

He laid his sights on a tree not far away and remembered that Owl told him to get up a tree at every opportunity, so Itty-Bitty scrambled up that tree. Immediately, he understood. The air was fresh up there, and Bitty rested for a moment. The building was clearer now, and Bitty set goals for the next few trees along the way; and while he was at it, he looked for hawks above and snakes below. He didn't see anything dangerous, but Owl said to stay in the shadows, so he did.

He continued on in the stinky, smelly hole, following the setting sun. At one point, his alert ears heard a scurrying sound nearby. He hid for a while in what seemed like a tiny cave (it was really a large can that once had beans in it) until two small mice scampered by, looking for food and shelter as it was getting dark. Bitty made it to the last tree and flew up it. He was in dire need of fresh air.

To his amazement, he was halfway there. He wanted to keep going, but it was nearly night, and Bitty had no desire to be in the stinky muck in the dark as he was already hearing rustling, slithering, gurgling, scary things. So he slept in that tree even though his tummy growled, his tail still hurt, and the fleas were itching him terribly. As dawn broke, Bitty decided he was going to get to that building as quickly and easily as possible.

Growl!!

So without looking around, Bitty hustled down the tree and started toward the building. Once again, in and around, zigzagging through the stink and muck. He was making good time and feeling like he was almost there, when all of a sudden, around the last corner he took, was the biggest, steepest, yuckiest, most fearsome mound in the landfill. "Oh, come on," Bitty yelled. He was mad! "Why does *everything* have to be so hard? I'm just a little cat who wants a home with a nice lady who will give me *saucers of milk!*" He flopped down and felt like he might cry. He was so tired and hungry and very frustrated.

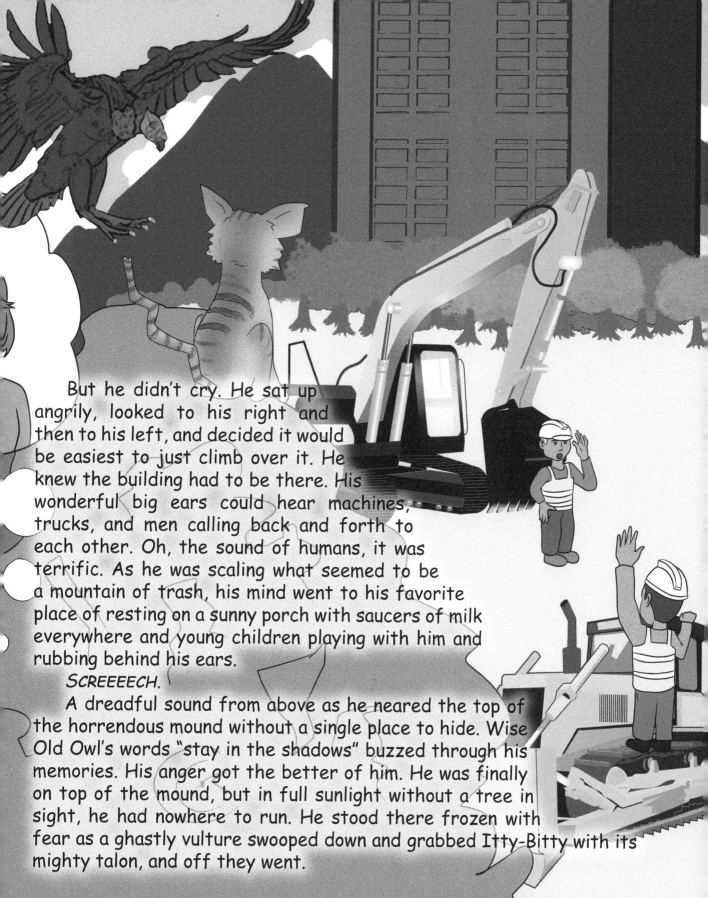

But he didn't cry. He sat up angrily, looked to his right and then to his left, and decided it would be easiest to just climb over it. He knew the building had to be there. His wonderful big ears could hear machines, trucks, and men calling back and forth to each other. Oh, the sound of humans, it was terrific. As he was scaling what seemed to be a mountain of trash, his mind went to his favorite place of resting on a sunny porch with saucers of milk everywhere and young children playing with him and rubbing behind his ears.

SCREEEEECH.

A dreadful sound from above as he neared the top of the horrendous mound without a single place to hide. Wise Old Owl's words "stay in the shadows" buzzed through his memories. His anger got the better of him. He was finally on top of the mound, but in full sunlight without a tree in sight, he had nowhere to run. He stood there frozen with fear as a ghastly vulture swooped down and grabbed Itty-Bitty with its mighty talon, and off they went.

22

Well, this is a fine mess I'm in, thought Itty-Bitty. *If I only took the time to go around...* He couldn't think about that right now. He had to think quickly. The ugly beast was about to fly right over the building on his way to his nest to enjoy his morning morsel. *No way!* thought Bitty. *If I can survive an alligator, a snake, a hawk, thunder and lightning, dozing foxes, and this never-ending stinking garbage pit, I can get out of this.* So he started clawing and biting at the talon, which the wicked winged monster didn't even notice. Then Itty-Bitty spied a spot on the talon that appeared to be an old wound, and if he bit hard enough, the hideous creature's talon just might let go.

23

So Bitty waited until they were just over the building's roof. Twisting his small lithe body, he bit as hard as he could into the soft spot. In a blink of an eye, Bitty was free and falling to the roof below. The annoyed foe circled around to collect his morsel. Luckily the roof was steep and slick from the recent rain and Itty-Bitty quickly slid down to the edge of the roof hanging on with his two front paws. The bird above missed his prey, and this time he gave up. The angry bird flew away defeated. *Oh no*, thought Bitty; he was losing his grip and began to fall. He quickly wrangled around to land on all four feet and hoped for the best. Miraculously, there was a human there watching the alarming event, and Bitty landed in her waiting arms. "Good catch, Fran," said one of the men nearby. It was too much for poor Bitty, and he conked out in the security of the human's arms.

A few minutes later, he awoke inside the building, and a caring lady was cleaning him up. "My, my," she said, "what kind of adventure have you had?" Bitty thought she would never believe him even if he could tell her. He looked at her with big adoring eyes and hoped she would be the nice lady who would take him home. Then she stuck him in a sink full of warm water.

Yikes, what is she doing? Doesn't she know cats hate water? Bitty thought maybe she wasn't so nice and, for a moment, thought another nicer lady would come along. Then he realized the muck and dirt and stink and fleas were all going away, and it felt wonderful. Oh, how he hoped she would be his new human.

Fran gently patted him dry and put him in a box she had in her office. Finally, she put a small plate of tuna and some cottage cheese in front of him, Bitty devoured it. Then Fran smiled at him and loosely closed the box so Bitty could rest, and rest he did.

The next thing he knew, he awoke with Fran and another young woman peering at him. "Oh my goodness," said the young lady, "look how cute he is. Look at his big ears and that tail—*wow*." Bitty had never been called cute or gushed about before, and he liked it.

"He's had an adventure," Fran said. "I wonder what happened to his tail."

The other girl picked him up and cuddled him. "Oh, Fran, I will take him to my mother—she will love him."

"Well, I would love to keep him, but I already have three cats, so okay, he's yours." Bitty's heart sank. He really liked Fran. All he could do now was hope the girl's mother was as kind as Fran had been. The young lady gave him some of her leftover lunch, and Bitty was off to sleep again.

The smell of something delicious woke Bitty from his sleep. He was in a new place, a lovely place, on a very lovely pillow on a very lovely chair with a very lovely blanket. "Oh look, Mom, he's awake." A sweet-looking older lady with red hair walked over to where Bitty was lounging comfortably.

"Oh, bless his heart," she said, smiling at him. She picked him up and placed him on her lap, where she began to rub behind his ears and neck.

   I must be dreaming, thought Itty-Bitty. Could it be that after all my hard work, my dream *finally* came true? *I have a home now? And a nice lady, Ms. Carol, who will take care of me?* Bitty was beyond happy. He was grateful and thought about Mama Wren, Nutty Squirrel, and most of all, Wise Old Owl who helped him so much. So thankful that Ms. Fran was there to catch him and care for him and to the young lady who brought him here to this wonderful family. As for all the other swamp creatures who teased him and offered no good words, he chose not to think about them at all because there, in the kitchen, was a saucer of milk given to him by a very nice lady!

About the Illustrator

Artist Mark Ziehr is cousin to Sharon Kitto-Rienstra. He has been drawing since the age of four and painting since age eleven. Mark lives in Austin, Texas, with his wife, Micka, of forty years. He has two sons, two lovely daughters-in-law, one delightful granddaughter, and four rough-and-tumble grandsons. Much of Mark's work can be seen on his website, www.zarthaus.com.

About the Author

Sharon Kitto-Rienstra is the author of the children's book series *Itty-Bitty Ditch Kitty*, which is based on a true story of a kitten that was found in a Carlyss, Louisiana, landfill and is the inspiration of the series that follows this young kitten who had to endure quite a journey through a swamp to find a loving home, then learn to get along with an aristocratic Siamese, help other lost animals in the neighborhood, and lastly, keep himself and his longtime friends healthy, stealthy, and wise in their older years. Sharon lives in Leander, Texas, with her husband, Rick, of thirty years and three kids—Drew, Lindsey, and Julie—nearby. Her parents, Carol and Bill Kitto, are featured characters in the series and were loving owners of the real Itty-Bitty throughout his life.